Secrets
of
Scary Fun

Other Young Yearling Books You Will Enjoy:
The Pee Wee Scouts books by Judy Delton

The Polka Dot Private Eye books by Patricia Reilly Giff

YEARLING BOOKS/YOUNG YEARLINGS/YEARLING CLASSICS are designed especially to entertain and enlighten young people. Patricia Reilly Giff, consultant to this series, received her bachelor's degree from Marymount College and a master's degree in history from St. John's University. She holds a Professional Diploma in Reading and a Doctorate of Humane Letters from Hofstra University. She was a teacher and reading consultant for many years, and is the author of numerous books for young readers.

For a complete listing of all Yearling titles,
write to Dell Readers Service,
P.O. Box 1045, South Holland, IL 60473.

THE
CREEPY
CREATURE
CLUB

Secrets
of
Scary Fun

Stephen Mooser

Illustrated by George Ulrich

A YOUNG YEARLING BOOK

Published by
Dell Publishing
a division of
Bantam Doubleday Dell Publishing Group, Inc.
666 Fifth Avenue
New York, New York 10103

ISBN: 0-440-40338-3

Printed in the United States of America

October 1990

10 9 8 7 6 5 4 3 2

CWO

For Kady Dalrymple

Contents

---- ◆ ----

Welcome!

This book is special. It's filled with all kinds of supersecret stuff. Just a few of the things you'll learn are: how to decorate a room like a Halloween nightmare, how to make a monster movie that you can carry around in your pocket, and how to brew up a monster feast. You'll also learn monster makeup, magic, and a few jokes too—scary ones, of course.

◆

The Creepy Creature Club
Secrets to Share

It was a gray and drizzly day. The Creepy Creatures, all ten of them, were in their clubhouse. Some of them were sitting on a long green couch beneath a giant spider twisting slowly on a string. Others were sitting on the floor twiddling their thumbs. All of them were bored.

For a long time no one spoke. Red-haired Ginger Stein scrunched up on the couch and went to sleep.

Finally, Rosa Dorado stood up and clapped her hands. She smiled and brushed back her long black hair.

"I bet other people get bored too," she said. "Let's give them something to do. We'll make a book. *The Creepy Creature Club Secrets of Scary Fun.*"

"Are you kidding!" said Henry Potter. As usual, his hair was sticking up in back.

Like a feather. "We can't tell our secrets."

"The Creepy Creatures believe in sharing," said Rosa. "I'm not afraid to share my secrets of scary makeup."

"And I'll tell everything I know about making monster movies," said Jody Grimes. She batted her eyelashes. "I want everyone to be in the movies. Like I was once ... almost."

"Well, I'm not telling a thing," said Henry. "I'm not telling anyone how I do my scary magic tricks. Anyone."

Rosa put a hand to her mouth. She pretended to yawn. "Then keep your silly secrets," she said. "We don't need them. Even without you I bet we can have the best book of scary fun ever."

"It won't be the best without my magic secrets," said Henry.

Rosa rolled her eyes. "We'll see about that." She handed little Melvin Purdy a pencil and a pad of paper.

"You're the best speller in the club," she said. "We'll tell you what to write down."

"This is going to be fun," said Melvin. He

3

wrote at the top of the page, "The Creepy Creature Club Secrets of Scary Fun."

"Now, if no one minds, I'll go first," said Rosa.

"And I won't go at all," said Henry. He folded his arms across his chest. "I don't tell secrets. In fact, in all the world no one can keep a secret better than me."

Rosa laughed. Henry wasn't the best secret-keeper. Only the biggest bragger. She shook her head, then turned to Melvin and began to share her secrets of scary makeup.

Chapter 1

◆

Rosa's Secrets of Scary Makeup: Blood, Scars, and Fangs

Blood, scars, and fangs! Is that the name of a new rock group? No. It's the contents of a monster's makeup kit. In this chapter I'll show you how to quickly turn yourself into the ugliest kid on the block. When you're a Creepy Creature, that's something to shoot for.

First, a word of caution. Before you use any makeup there are a few things you need to know:

1. Some people are allergic to certain

kinds of makeup. If anything you put on your skin gives you a rash, don't use it again.

2. Don't ever put anything on your lips or in your mouth.
3. Don't ever put anything in your eyes.
4. Use cold cream to wash off makeup. Afterward you can remove the cold cream with warm water and soap.
5. No matter what the project, clean up your mess when you are done.

Scars

Lipstick-and-Eyeliner Scar

The easiest scar to make requires just two things: red lipstick and black eyeliner. Borrow them from your mother, an older sister, or a friend.

Use the red lipstick to draw a thin line on your cheek. Use the eyeliner to draw a line under the lipstick mark. Then, again using the eyeliner, crosshatch the lipstick. Like this:

Clean up later using cold cream, warm water, and soap.

Rubber-Cement Scar

This is another easy scar to make. To make this scar you'll need a bottle of rubber cement and some red or purple food coloring.

Begin by pouring a thick line of rubber cement onto a piece of glass or a mirror.

Color the cement with a few drops of food coloring.

Let it dry. This will take from a few minutes to a half hour.

Finally, peel it off the glass. It should be sticky enough to put right on your cheek.

Gelatin Scars

If you want to look like a zombie, or if you prefer big, huge, jagged scars, then you may want to make a gelatin scar. They're not hard to make. All you need is red, purple, or green food coloring and a box of unflavored gelatin. You can buy both ingredients at the market.

First decide how much of your face you

want covered with slime. For a small scar one teaspoon of gelatin will do. Three teaspoons will give you enough to cover your cheek.

Next put a teaspoonful or more of the gelatin into a small bowl.

For each teaspoon of gelatin add one teaspoon of hot water from the faucet. Then stir.

Add a few drops of your favorite awful color. Then stir some more.

When it is cool enough to touch (about a minute), dab it onto your face with your finger. Paint on extra layers if you want it to be thick.

Remember, keep all makeup and other materials away from your eyes and mouth.

Let it dry.

Now go out and scare someone silly.

A gelatin scar can be peeled off easily. Wash off any remaining bits and pieces with warm water and soap.

Finally, clean up your bowls and spoons.

Fangs

Fangs make a lovely addition to any Creepy Creature. And, of course, vampires wouldn't be caught dead without them.

If you're lazy you can buy plastic fangs in the toy department of most stores. If you're too lazy even to go to the store, here's how to make fangs at home.

Get an empty milk carton. Cut out a large square.

Draw a pattern like this:

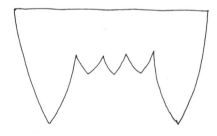

onto the clean white surface of the carton.

Cut out the fangs.

Place the fangs between your top lip and your gums. Cackle madly. Congratulations! You've just turned yourself into a vampire.

Blood

Some people can't stand the sight of blood. That's probably why Creepy Creatures love it so much. Of course, you must never use the real thing. So when your outfit for the evening calls for a dash of blood, why not choose one of these delightful recipes:

Poster Paint

Drip a bit of red poster paint onto your hand, neck, or face, but *never* in or near your eyes, mouth, or lips. It looks a lot like dried blood. And it's easy to wash off with warm water and soap.

Catsup

I'm sure you've used catsup before as blood. It can look very real, but it does have problems. It doesn't dry, so it can be quite runny. Also, it can stain clothes. When using catsup be sure you have on old clothes.

Flour and Syrup

Clear Karo syrup, red food coloring, and flour make excellent blood. Pour a little syrup into a bowl. Mix in an equal amount of flour. Add food coloring. This fake blood looks as real as catsup but isn't runny. Wash it off with soap and warm water.

Chapter 2

◆

Make Your Own Monster Movie

"**L**et me go next," said Jody. She smiled, showing off her new braces. "I want to tell everyone how to make scary monster movies."

"Fine," said Rosa. "Chapter two will be just for you."

Henry Potter shook his head. "I don't believe it. You're giving away all our secrets."

"We're just sharing," said Rosa. "If you don't want to share that's all right. You just won't be in the book."

Henry laughed. "Who cares about your silly book," he said. "Certainly not me."

Rosa nodded. "Good," she said. "Go ahead, Jody. Tell us your secrets of making

12

monster movies. When everybody reads the book you'll be famous." She took a long look at Henry. "Not like some people I know."

Jody's Monster Movie Secrets

Monster movies cost millions of dollars to make. I'd like to show you how to make one for a dollar or less. Best of all, you won't need a camera to make it. Or a projector to show it. And you can carry it around in your pocket!

Sound impossible? Hardly. Please, step into the Creepy Creature Film Studio. I'll show you how to make some great super-low-budget monster flicks.

Flip Pictures

Flip pictures have been around nearly as long as paper. (There's even one running along the bottom of this book. Grab some popcorn, flip through the pages, and enjoy the show.)

Maybe you've even made a flip picture yourself. They're really quite simple.

To make your first monster movie epic you'll need a pack of twenty-five or more 3×5 white cards and a pen that uses black ink.

Hold the cards in your hand. Thumb through them as if they were a pack of playing cards. Notice how, as the cards flip by, you can clearly see the edge of the card. The area that you can see is where you will draw your movie. By using each corner, front and back, you will have room for four flip movies.

To get you started, let's make the first flip movie together. This frightening film we'll call *Revenge of the Giant Foot*.

At the top edge of your top card, draw the bottom of a giant foot. Below it, at the very bottom of the card, draw a house or two. Keep the pictures simple. Details won't show up. What's most important is the story and the action.

On the next card draw the foot a little farther down. You have a lot of cards so don't move it too far, just a little bit each time. Slowly, show the foot coming down toward the houses. Toward the last of your cards (maybe six or seven cards from the end) the foot will begin to hit the houses. Till then the houses should be the same in each picture. For the last few cards show the foot crunching into the houses. Have pieces of wood fly up into the air. Have dust rise.

When you have finished your twenty-five or so drawings, flip through the cards. The giant foot should appear to smash the houses.

Congratulations. You've just made your first monster movie. Keep it up and soon you'll be winning Oscars.

Making More Monster Movies

If you want to be a success in show business you'll have to make more than one movie. Think up more ideas for flip movies. Remember, keep everything simple. These are a few of the films the Creepy Creatures have made. Try them yourself if you want.

The Shrinking Nightmare

A smiling face suddenly starts to shrink. As it shrinks the smile turns to a scream. Start on the top card with a large, smiling face. Make the face smaller as you go through the cards. Change the smile to a scream. Make the eyes round. Have the hair stand on end. Try this same film in reverse. Put the tiny face on top. Put the big, smiling face on the bottom. Incredible! You've just made two monster movies for the price of one!

Attack of the Shark

A smiling shark opens his jaws, then clamps them shut. By the middle of your flip pack of cards the shark's jaws and sharp teeth should fill the picture. For an extra-scary touch have the shark bite down on an arm.

Birth of the Thing

A dot starts to grow. It sprouts ten legs. Two antennas shoot out of its head. Giant, bulging eyes appear atop the antennas. Start with a circle the size of a dime in the middle of the card. Expand the circle to the size of a quarter. Then make the legs and antennas appear. Do it all slowly, half a leg at a time. The antennas can grow at the same time, the eyeballs at the end. If possible, have the legs wiggle. It will give your film a nice, creepy touch.

Chapter 3

◆

Ginger's Ugly Spider

"**W**ho's next?" asked Rosa. She looked around the room. Everyone was raising his hand. Everyone but Henry. He was sitting in the middle of the couch playing with a deck of cards. Atop his head was a tall, shiny magic hat.

"Henry, you're wearing your magic costume," said Rosa. "Does this mean you're going to share your secrets of scary magic? Have you changed your mind?"

Henry turned the cards into a fan. He fanned his face. "I'm thinking about it," he said.

"You'd better think fast," said Rosa. "Whoever writes the best chapter will get his picture on the cover."

"Really?" said Henry.

"Really," said Rosa. "But I know you don't care about being famous. Do you?"

Henry gulped. "Well ..."

"All you care about is keeping your secrets," said Rosa. She pointed at Ginger Stein. "Ginger, why don't you tell everyone your secrets of making monster mobiles."

"Gladly," said Ginger. Her curly red hair bounced as she got up from the couch. "Just watch. I'm going to write the best chapter ever. Then I'll be on the cover of the book."

Henry tipped his hat and grinned. "Not so fast, Ginger. Don't you think this handsome face would look better on the front of our book?"

"To be on the cover you have to share your secrets," said Rosa. "I thought you didn't want to share."

"Well," said Henry. He cleared his throat. Then shuffled the cards. "I might tell some. Just a few."

Rosa shook a finger at Henry. "You have to tell them all," she said. "Anyway, put your hat back on your head. It's Ginger's

A Giant Creepy Creature Spider

Hanging from the rafters of the Creepy Creature clubhouse is a giant spider. He's big. He's ugly. And he scares everyone who stops by. No wonder we Creepy Creatures like him so much.

If you, too, would like to welcome your guests by saying, "Come in. Make yourselves uncomfortable," then perhaps you should make a giant spider to decorate your room. It's not that hard to do.

All you'll need is:

> Newspaper
> One bag of flour
> Two balloons (one large, one half the size)
> Scissors
> White glue
> Two large bowls of water
> Poster paints and brush

You have probably worked with papier-mâché before. If so, you know it can be quite messy. Before you begin, pick a place to work. An outside table would be best. If you are going to work inside, make sure you put down lots of newspaper before you begin. It's also a good idea to put on old clothes. You want your mom to scream when she sees the spider—not when she sees the mess you've made.

Now set out all the ingredients.

First blow up the two balloons. The large one will serve as a mold for the spider's body. The small one will serve as the head. So make sure the big balloon is about three times bigger.

Next tear one-half- to one-inch-wide strips of newspaper. Make the strips as long as the length of the page. Do about twenty pages. (If you find you need more you can tear them later.) Tear some of the strips in half crosswise. You can use these to cover smaller spaces.

Fill one large bowl with water. This bowl will be used to wash your hands as you work.

Take out the other bowl and mix up the papier-mâché paste. Put in three cups of flour and two to two and one-half cups of water. Add a spoonful of white glue, if you wish. Experiment. You want your paste to be like thick soup. Mix it up with your hands. Squeeze out all lumps.

Begin applying the papier-mâché. Pick up a strip of newspaper. Dip it into the paste. Pull it through your fingers to squeeze out the extra paste.

Then lay the sticky paper strip on the large balloon. Wrap it around. Press it down. Squeeze out any lumps. Lay the next strip down crosswise. Repeat. Keep going till the whole balloon is covered. After you have finished one layer, do another. Keep going till you have covered the balloon with four layers of newspaper strips. Add a fifth layer of extra-big strips if you wish to get a nice smooth surface.

Remember: Alternate the way you lay down the strips. First put one lengthwise. Next put one crosswise.

When you have finished the large balloon, set it aside to dry.

Take a short break and wash your hands in the bowl of water.

Now take the small balloon—the spider's head—and cover it with papier-mâché too. After you have put on two layers, stop.

The head must be made just a little differently. You have to add a knob at the back of the head. That's so you can attach it to the body. Also, you need to add some lumps near the top of the head for eyes.

Add the knob by wadding up some paper. Get it wet if you wish. Stick it on the back of the balloon. Then cover it with two more layers of papier-mâché strips. Make the eyes the same way. Wad up a small amount of paper. Make the wad the size of a Ping-Pong ball or smaller. Stick the wads on the top of your first two layers where you want the eyes to go. Then finish covering the balloon with two or three more layers of strips.

Set the small balloon aside to dry.

The spider's legs are easy to make. Take eight full pages of newspaper. Take each page, one by one, and twist it from top to bottom. When done, you will have made eight long, skinny legs.

Dip each leg in the paste. Make sure the paste gets all the way through the paper.

24

Curve each leg so that, when attached to the body, it will look like a real spider's leg.

Set the eight legs aside to dry.

Clean up your mess. Wash out all bowls. Put away all ingredients. Throw out any extra paper. Wash your hands.

Papier-mâché needs two to three days to dry. Shorter if it's outside on a sunny day. Longer if inside on a shelf.

After the papier-mâché has dried, lay down newspaper and bring out the scissors, the paint, and the white glue.

Poke four small holes in each side of the large balloon. These holes will be where you will place the spider's legs. Don't worry about popping the balloon inside. The dried papier-mâché will keep its shape.

Cut a larger hole at the top front of the large balloon. This is where you will fit the knob at the back of the spider's head.

Fit the legs and the head into the proper holes. Use lots of white glue (or more papier-mâché newspaper and paste) to hold everything in place. Then let dry.

Paint your spider any way you want. Use poster paints for easiest cleanup. Paint the eyes a bright color.

Fangs can either be painted on or cut from cardboard. If cut from stiff cardboard, glue them onto the spider's jaw with white glue.

Clean up.

Finally, put a small hook or paper clip into the center of the spider's back. Then have someone help you hang him by a piece of dark thread from a hook in the ceiling.

"Congratulations!" said Ginger. "You've decorated your room. Now bring over your friends and say, "Step inside. Please. Make yourselves uncomfortable.""

Chapter 4

More Monster Mobiles

"My turn! My turn!" said Henry. He jumped up and began waving his magic hat in the air. "I'm ready to talk."

"Whoa! Wait a minute," said Ginger. "I'm not done. I want to tell everyone how to make more scary mobiles."

Henry glared at Ginger. "Some people want to hog the whole book."

"A second ago you didn't even want to be in the book," said Melvin.

"A second ago was before he found out he could be on the cover," said Rosa. "Henry, why do you always have to be such a big shot?"

"Big shot?" said Henry. "Why, I'm the most modest guy in the world."

Rosa laughed. Everyone did.

"I just want to share my secrets now. That's all," said Henry. He winked and pointed a finger at Rosa. "Hey, Henry Potter is a sharing kind of guy."

"Then you won't mind sharing your time with Ginger," said Rosa. "She isn't finished."

Henry took off his hat and gave Ginger a big bow. "Go ahead," he said. "Tell us some more about monster mobiles."

"Gladly," said Ginger.

Ginger's Spider Mobile

If you'd like some more spiders hanging around your room, then you're going to need a monster mobile.

To make a mobile you'll need:

> String
> Scissors
> Cotton
> Cardboard
> Some sticks, coat hangers, or wooden dowels
> Crayons or poster paint

To make your mobile frame you need to use one twelve-inch stick and two six-inch sticks. Mom or Dad can get these sticks at the hardware store. They will even cut them for you. Or you can get Mom or Dad or another adult to cut up metal coat hangers into the right lengths.

Attach a two-foot string to the center of the longest stick.

Then attach shorter, six-inch strings to the ends of the long stick.

Hang the shorter sticks off the end of the long stick. Attach the string to the middle of the short sticks.

Next prepare five scary things that you will hang from your mobile.

The five things will hang like this:

Use your imagination. Almost anything can be hung from the mobile. Cut a ghost shape from an old rag. Paint a scary face on a Christmas ornament. Or use old, broken dolls. At Halloween time there are lots of creepy things to buy. Paper spiders, pumpkins, witches, skulls, and ghosts all can be hung from your mobile. Mix and match. There is no rule that says all the objects have to be the same.

Make up your own designs. Trace them out on stiff cardboard. Or, if you wish, trace some of these designs:

Cut out your designs.
Color them in.

Poke a small hole in the top of your design. Thread some string through the hole. Then attach it to the ends of the small sticks. Attach one to the center of the big stick.

Make sure everything balances. If it doesn't, move the strings or add a paper clip for extra weight. Mobiles look best when everything hangs evenly.

Finally, get Mom or Dad or another adult to hang your latest Creepy Creature creation from a hook in the ceiling.

"Now is your room creepy enough?" said Ginger. "If not, go on to the next chapter. But do it only if you're brave. Only if you're not afraid of graveyards, ghosts, and zombies."

Chapter 5

Monsters That Move

"**G**inger, that was great," said Henry. He jumped up and took Ginger's place alongside Melvin. "Now let's talk about magic." After pushing his top hat back with his finger he raised a single eyebrow. "Quick, someone. Take a picture. We'll use it on the cover of the book."

Rosa shook her head. "Sorry, Henry. But Ollie is going next. He's going to tell us how to make a zombie and a ghost."

"A zombie and a ghost that really move," said little Ollie Morton in a squeaky voice. He had big ears and a tiny nose. He giggled. "I hope this part of the book doesn't scare too many people."

"Whoa, wait a minute," said Henry. He put his hands on his hips. "I thought I was next."

THE
END

"Wait your turn," said Rosa. "We'll put you in the book . . . if there's room."

"What!" said Henry. "What do you mean, if there's room?"

"Henry, you're impossible," said Rosa. "First you don't want to be in the book. Now you won't let anyone else be in it."

"I didn't say Ollie couldn't be in it. I just wanted to go ahead of him," said Henry. He looked around the room. "What do you say, pals, can I go next?"

Everyone shook his head no.

Henry raised his hands. "I get it," he said. "You want to save the best for last."

"Henry, why don't you show us a magic trick right now," said Rosa.

Henry grinned. "Really? Which one?"

"Let's see you disappear," said Rosa. "And give Ollie his turn."

Everyone laughed. Henry sighed and sat down on the couch. And Ollie Morton stood up and began to share his secrets.

Ollie's Zombie and Ghost

For years mad scientists in books and movies have been building monsters. Now here's a chance for you to build some yourself. It's easier than you think. Please, won't you step into the Creepy Creature laboratory. We can begin at once.

Building a Zombie

Zombies are people who have returned from the grave. They look human, almost. Their clothes are usually ripped and dirty. And their faces are a real mess. Making a zombie requires only a few old clothes. With luck you should have everything in a rag drawer, or ask Mom or Dad for some old clothes. Make sure they're no longer needed. To make your zombie you'll need:

> Old long-sleeve shirt
> Old pants
> Pair of gloves
> Pair of socks
> Hat or cap
> 15–20 safety pins
> Old pillowcase
> Scary Halloween mask (optional)
> Pile of old newspapers, rags, or a
>   small ball
> Poster paint or felt-tipped pens

To make the zombie you must stuff the clothes with wadded-up newspapers. Then clip everything together using the safety pins.

First stuff the pillowcase. For stuffing use either the newspapers, rags, or a ball. Tie the bottom in a knot. The pillowcase will be the zombie's head.

Use the optional scary mask or paint on an ugly face. The uglier, the better. Use poster paint or felt-tipped pens.

Now stuff the other pieces of clothing. Use rags or paper to stuff the pants, the shirt, the socks, and the gloves.

Pin everything together. Use the safety pins to attach the socks to the pants, then to attach the pants to the shirt. Pin the gloves to the ends of the sleeves. Finally, pin the hat onto the head and then pin the head onto the shirt.

Splash some red poster paint onto the clothes. Remember, your zombie just stepped from the grave. Make him look that way.

Soon you will learn how to make your creature move. But first ... let's make a ghost.

Building a Ghost

All you need to make your ghost is: an old sheet, poster paint or felt-tipped pens, a few sheets of newspaper, and three rubber bands.

First get the sheet. Make sure it is one that is no longer needed.

Next wad up the newspapers into a ball about the size of a head.

Lay out the sheet on the floor. Place the wadded up "head" in the center of the sheet.

Wrap the sheet around the head. Place the rubber band over the head. Tighten it around the ghost's neck.

Pinch the corners of the head to make ears. Put rubber bands under the ears to hold them in place.

Finally, paint on a ghostly face. Big circles for eyes and a wide, screaming mouth may look best.

You now should have a ghost that looks like this:

Your ghost is finished. Introduce him to the zombie. They're going to be good friends. Good neighbors, actually. They'll both be "living" in the place you're going to build next, your very own graveyard!

An Instant Boneyard

Your Creepy Creature cemetery needs two or more graves. One will be for the ghost. The other is for the zombie. The easiest grave will be one made from an empty cardboard box.

Get two or more clean, empty boxes at least twelve inches high and two feet square. Make sure the boxes have flaps.

Draw a tombstone on the front of the box. Write something on the tombstone. Something like:

Bad Bill
1802–1835

or

R.I.P.
Weird Willie
Gone but not forgotten

or

No-Nose Kate
1854–1892
Once I wasn't
Then I was
Now I ain't again

Or make up your own, the creepier the better.

40

Making Your Monsters Move

To bring your creatures to life you'll need two round hooks and some heavy black thread or string.

Tie one end of the thread to your monster's head or neck.

You are going to make your creatures rise from their graves. To do this you need to put two round hooks in the ceiling. Have Mom or Dad or another adult help you screw them in. The hooks should be above the boxes.

Place the zombie in one box. Put the ghost in another box. Lightly close the flaps.

Next take the black strings that are tied to the monsters and thread them through the hooks. Get an adult to help you.

Move away from the boxes. When you pull on the threads the creatures will appear to rise from their graves.

Practice bringing your creepy friends to life. Experiment with the lighting. If you can't see the string it will be even scarier.

Invite everyone over to meet your new pals. Why not give them a real show? In the next chapter the Creepy Creatures will give you some ideas for the show. Some of the plays are scary. Some are funny. All of them, of course, are a real scream.

Chapter 6

◆

Putting on a Scary Play

"**T**hanks, Ollie," said Rosa. "Who wants to go next? Who wants to share their secrets of scary fun?"

Henry Potter's hand shot up like a rocket. "Potter the Great is ready to take the stage!" he yelled. "Gangway. Prepare to learn the greatest, scariest magic tricks ever!"

Rosa yawned and tapped Melvin on the shoulder.

"Sorry, Henry, but Melvin wants to go next."

"Huh?" said Melvin. He shook his head. "But I didn't raise my hand."

"That's right," said Henry. "No one raised his hand but me. Come on. Let me share my secrets."

Rosa shook her head. "Sorry, Henry. This

43

next chapter doesn't call for a magician. It calls for a writer. We need some plays for the zombie and the ghost to act in."

"We do?" said Melvin.

"We certainly do," said Rosa. "And you're the man for the job. You're the best writer in the club."

Melvin gulped. "But where do I begin?"

"At the beginning, of course," said Rosa. "Isn't that where a good story always starts?"

"Yes, but—"

"No buts," said Rosa. "Begin."

Melvin looked at Rosa and sighed. He knew there was no point in arguing. So he did as Rosa wished. He began.

Melvin's Creepy Creature Theater

You've made your monsters. Now let's put them to work! How about using them in a play? You can write your own. Or use the one in this chapter. You'll find a play in the next chapter too. It stars your next creepy creation, the invisible woman.

45

First, before the curtain goes up, you need to do some planning. Pick a place to put on the play. Make sure there is room for your actors. And make sure there is room for your audience too.

Decorate the room. Hang your monster mobiles and your big spider from the ceiling. Find some scary music to play. Or make up the scary sounds and record them on a tape recorder. Fill the tape with moans and cackles and screams. Blow on an empty bottle to make a low, moaning sound. Crinkling up cellophane sounds like a fire. Rattling a stiff piece of cardboard sounds like thunder. Experiment. Then play the music as your guests arrive for the play.

Make up tickets. Like everything else, have them look scary. Something like this, perhaps:

Make up posters too. If you wish, charge something for the play. A dollar or fifty cents, perhaps. The money you make can help pay for your next play. Like your tickets, make the poster scary. Let people know what the play is, where it will be, and the time it will start.

How about selling refreshments? It would be a nice way to make some extra money at the play. Invent scary names for your snacks. For instance, you can sell cherry juice and call it Dracula's Delight. Or sell black licorice and call it Candy Snakes.

47

On the day of the play make sure everything is ready. Have the refreshments out. Check to make sure the lights are working. Set out all the chairs. Everyone working in the theater should wear a costume. Make sure your guests have a good time. You'll want them to come back again and again.

Make up your own plays. Or use this one:

Play Idea: The Laughing Ghost

Setting: The graveyard.

Characters: A zombie, a ghost, an announcer.

[You will need two people to control the strings on your characters. You will also need two people to read the parts of the zombie and the ghost. Have the actors hide near the graveyard, maybe behind a couch. Make sure they can see the zombie and the ghost as they read. The zombie and the ghost should jiggle whenever they speak.]

Announcer: It's comedy night at the graveyard! I'm sure you'll agree, to-night's comedians are a real scream. First, let me introduce someone you don't get to see often. Ghost!

[The ghost should slowly come up out of the box.]

Ghost: Glad to be here. If you like the show be sure to boo. It's my favorite sound.

Announcer: And now, here he is, straight from the grave, it's a Zombie!

[The zombie now comes slowly out of the box.]

Zombie: What a great audience. You all look half-dead! My favorite kind of people.

Ghost: Hey, Zombie. I can't get my friend, the skeleton, to laugh. What should I do?

Zombie: Tickle his funny bone!

Ghost: Say, what did you think of Dracula's party?

Zombie: It was okay, but there were too many vampires there. Those guys bug me.

Ghost: How come?

Zombie: I guess it's because vampires are such pains in the neck.

Ghost: Speaking of vampires, do you know why they all have such sharp teeth?

Zombie: No. I don't know why their teeth are so sharp.

Ghost: Forget it. You wouldn't get the point.

Zombie: That joke is just like the one about the roof.

Ghost: What's the roof joke?

Zombie: Forget it. It's over your head.

Ghost: Very funny. But seriously, I've been wondering. Why do zombies always stand in the very middle of the room?

Zombie: Because it's their favorite spot, the dead center. [pause] Now let me ask you a question.

Ghost: Shoot.

Zombie: Don't tempt me.

Ghost: What's the question?

Zombie: How does a dumb ghost like you stay in school?

Ghost: Because they need me. I'm the school spirit.

Zombie: Sure you are. And Count Dracula is the batboy for the New York Yankees.

Ghost: Speaking of baseball, let's play a game. Can you dig up some friends?

Zombie: Sure. Just give me a shovel.

Ghost: Yuck. I think I'd better be going. My mummy is calling. She needs help.

Zombie: Help? Can't your mummy help herself?

Ghost: Not right now. My mummy is all tied up. So, so long, Zombie. When I get home I'll give you a call.

Zombie: Don't bother. My phone is always dead.

[The ghost and zombie should slowly settle back into their boxes.]

Zombie: Thanks for coming.

Ghost: Good-bye. If you liked the show please boo.

The End

There are lots of other things you can do with your zombie and ghost. Write more plays. And this time mix in live actors. Or put on a tape and have the monsters dance and sing. Or lip-synch to a tape and use your creepy creations as a backup group.

As always, use your imagination. Remember, it's a monster play. So the worse, the better.

Chapter 7

◆

Starring the Invisible Woman

"**T**hat was wonderful," said Rosa. "Maybe Melvin should be on the cover of our book."

Melvin slicked down his hair. He grinned. "Really? Me? Little old Melvin Purdy?"

"That last chapter was awfully good," said Rosa.

"If you think that was good, wait till you hear what I have to say," said Henry. He stood up and waved his pack of cards. "Ladies and gentlemen, presenting—"

"Melvin Purdy!" shouted Melvin, raising his fist. "That was so much fun I want to write another play."

Henry groaned. "Another play!"

"This one is going to be even better than the last one," said Melvin. "It's going to be all about the invisible woman."

"A play about an invisible woman!" said Henry. "This I've got to see."

Melvin wiggled his eyebrows. "You mean, 'This I've got to *can't* see.' Don't forget, the star is invisible."

Everyone laughed at Melvin's joke. Everyone but Henry.

"Go on," said Henry, sitting back down. "But this better be good."

"It will be," said Melvin.

And it was.

Melvin Presents the Invisible Woman

If you built the zombie, then building the invisible woman will be easy. And why not? Most of her can't even be seen.

For your invisible woman you will need:

Hat or cap
Short-sleeve blouse

Skirt

(Make sure these clothes are no longer needed.)

Two coat hangers

Heavy black thread or string

8–10 safety pins

Old shoes or sandals (optional)

Attach the end of the thread to the top of one of the coat hangers. Drape the skirt over the coat hanger.

Bend down the top of the second coat hanger. Then hang the blouse over it. No part of the coat hanger should show.

Use the safety pins to fasten the blouse to the skirt. Thread the string up through the blouse. Wrap it securely around the center of the coat hanger. Then pull it out through the neck.

About one foot above the neck of the blouse, loop the thread around a safety pin and tie it off. Then continue to thread the string through the top of the hat or cap. You may need to get help putting the string through the cap. Ask Mom or Dad to help you put it through with a needle. The hat will rest on the safety pin.

Shoes can also be added to your invisible woman. Attach black string to the ends of the coat hanger in the skirt. A foot or so beneath the bottom of the skirt, tie on shoes or sandals.

Ask an adult to run the string that comes out of the hat up to a ring screwed into the ceiling. If possible use the hooks already in place for your ghost and zombie.

Pull up on the string. Your invisible woman will come to life. Once she is standing, adjust the clothes till she looks real.

The invisible woman will look best in a dimly lit room. The harder it is to see the string, the more real she will be.

Now that your latest creation is complete, why not show her off? Jerk her up and down and make her do the latest dance. Add her to your Creepy Creature singing group. Or put her in a play. Write your own. Or use this one. The Creepy Creatures put it on last year. It's called:

The Invisible Woman and the Doctor

Setting: A doctor's office. A desk and a chair.

Characters: A doctor, an assistant to the doctor, and the invisible woman.

[Besides the invisible woman you will need someone hidden nearby to read her lines. You also need someone to work the string holding her and to make sure her clothes jerk slightly as she speaks her lines.]

[As the play opens, the invisible woman should be folded up on the floor next to the doctor's desk. The assistant (male or female) will be standing next to the doctor's desk—the doctor can be either male or female too. It all depends on who wants to act in your play. The lights should be off or very dim. To begin the play turn up the lights.]

Assistant: Doctor, the invisible woman is here to see you.

Doctor: [Shuffling through some papers on her desk. She doesn't look up.] Tell the invisible woman I can't see her.

Assistant: Well, neither can I. Still I think you should talk to her.

Doctor: Oh, all right. Send her in.

[Pull up the invisible woman. The doctor and the assistant should be surprised to see her appear so suddenly.]

Doctor: Nice to not see you again. What's your problem this time?

Invisible Woman: Everyone laughs at me. Do you think I'm ugly?

Doctor: No, but let's face it. You're not much to look at.

Invisible Woman: I may not be much to look at, but I do have lots of friends.

Assistant: [Whispering to the audience.] Friends? I can't imagine what they see in her.

Doctor: Just how many friends do you have, Invisible Woman?

Invisible Woman: Hundreds, maybe thousands.

Doctor: I don't believe you for a second. That's a lie, isn't it?

Invisible Woman: Yes. How did you know?

Doctor: Because I can see right through you.

Invisible Woman: So, tell me, Doctor, what's your opinion? Am I crazy?

Doctor: Well, I will say this. You're certainly not all there.

Assistant: [Whispering to the audience.] Poor thing. She's really missing out on a lot.

61

THE
END

Invisible Woman: Before I go, tell me, am I all right?

Doctor: Better than all right.

Invisible Woman: Really?

Doctor: Yep. No doubt about it, Invisible Woman. You are totally out of sight!

Invisible Woman: Thank you. I've got to go now. But I hope to see you again soon.

Doctor: I hope you do see me soon. But I know I'll never see you again.

Invisible Woman: You won't?

Doctor: Of course not. If I saw you you wouldn't be the invisible woman. Right?

Assistant: [As the lights go out.] Hmmm. That's something to think about.

The End

Chapter 8

◆

Monster Magic

"**W**ho's next?" asked Rosa.

No one raised his hand. Not even Henry.

"Have you changed your mind?" asked Rosa, looking at Henry. "I thought you wanted to share your magic secrets."

"I do," said Henry. "But I thought you would never call on me. Is it really my turn?"

"It is, but I want you to share everything," said Rosa. "Don't leave anything out."

"Can I leave out the floating-finger trick?" asked Henry. "It's my favorite."

"Keep it out if you want," said Rosa. "But just remember this: The one who shares the most gets to be on the cover."

Henry bit his lip and thought. At last he stood up and took a bow.

"Ladies and gentlemen," he said. "Presenting Henry Potter's Secrets of Scary Magic!"

"Presenting all of them?" asked Rosa.

Henry winked. "That's one secret this magician will never tell."

And then he began.

Henry's Secrets of Scary Magic

Anyone who can create an invisible woman probably doesn't need magic lessons. Still, I've included a few magic tricks here. It's always fun to amaze your friends. And the Creepy Creatures guarantee these tricks will do just that.

Remember, magic is like everything else. The more you practice, the better you will be. Practice your tricks before you show them to your friends. Make people believe you really can work magic.

Magicians do more than just magic. They put on a whole show. Wear a costume. If you don't have a magician's costume, make one up. Wear all black, for instance. Black pants and a black shirt make a fine costume. If you can also find some white gloves, all the better. Besides practicing your tricks, practice what you are going to say. The best magic show is usually the one that is best rehearsed.

To warm up your audience you may want to ask some riddles. Try this one to help get your audience in a mood to be amazed:

Question: Two werewolves were born on the same day in the same year. They have the same mother and father. But they're not twins. How come?

Answer: They have a brother born on the same day. They're triplets!

Two Simple Card Tricks

You will need a deck of cards and the box they came in.

Trick Number One: The Floating Card

In this trick a card will seem to mysteriously rise out of a box of cards.

Here's how it is done: Before the magic show begins, cut a one-inch-square hole in the center of the back of the card box.

Then, when your audience is seated, pull out the box of cards. Hold it up. Open the top. Then announce that you have a box of magic cards. Command one of them to rise. The card at the very back is the one that will rise. So if you want to name the card, place it in the back before the show.

"King of spades!" you can say. "Come out and say hello."

To make the card rise, put your thumb or one of your other fingers into the hole and push up.

Practice this before you try it out in front of an audience. Don't let anyone see the back of the deck. After you are done, pull all the cards out of the box and go on to the next trick. Put the box away.

Trick Number Two: A Magic Flip

In this trick a person picks a card. He looks at it but doesn't let you see it. Then he puts it back in the deck. When you spread out the deck of cards facedown, one card is faceup. The card, of course, is the one the person picked.

Here's how it is done: Spread a deck of cards out on a table. Then have someone pick a card.

"Don't let me see it," you say.

While the person is looking at his card, gather up the remaining cards. As you do this turn the bottom card over. Then flip over the deck.

You might have to do this behind your back. But it will work best if you can do it while the person isn't looking.

Next have the person slide his card into the deck. You should be holding the deck in your hands.

Because you flipped the bottom card and then turned over the deck, only the person's card and the top card will be facedown. The rest of the deck is faceup. So be careful. Keep the cards tightly together.

Now put the cards behind your back. As you do, say the magic word, "Abracadabra!" Flip the card that you turned over before, the top one. When you have done this it will again be facing the same way as the other cards in the deck.

Finally, say "Shazam!" and spread out the cards, facedown. To your friend's surprise one card, his card, will be faceup.

Amazing!

Before you go on to your next trick why not tell another riddle? How about this one:

Question: My friend lives on the thirteenth floor of a tall building. Every day she goes to the sixth floor, then walks up the rest of the way. She wishes she could ride to her floor. But she can't, even though the elevator works fine. Why is it she can only go to the sixth floor?

Answer: Because she's just a little girl. And even on tiptoes she can only reach as high as the button for the sixth floor.

The Magic Chair

For the next part of the show bring out a straight-backed wooden chair.

"This is a magic chair," you announce. "Can I have a volunteer to test it out?"

When someone comes forward have him sit in the chair. Then say, "Put your feet together flat on the floor. Put your hands in your lap. Your back must touch the back of the chair."

Point to the chair and say some magic words. Then announce that the chair has the person in its power. That as long as he keeps his feet on the floor and his back straight against the chair, he can't stand. And he can't! It's impossible.

When he finally gives up, call someone else to the front for your final magic trick. Pick someone who was laughing at the person who couldn't stand.

Tell your new volunteer to sit in the chair. Then say the chair has put him under your power. He will now have to do whatever you tell him to do.

"Oh, yeah," the person will probably say. "I'm not going to do what you tell me."

"I think you will," you should reply. "My command to you is this: Get out of the chair!"

If the person wants to spend the rest of the day sitting in the chair, he can. But he will probably soon get up, obeying your command!

A Final Riddle

Question: What kind of music do mummies like best?

Answer: Wrap music, of course.

A Grand Finale

"Speaking of rapping," you might say, "it's time, as the mummy maker says, to wrap this thing up."

At this point challenge the audience to match wits with you.

"Some of you still might not believe I'm the world's greatest magician," you can say. "Well, here is a final trick to prove my skill."

At this point hold up some sheets of eight-and-one-half-by-eleven-inch paper. Make sure there is a piece for everyone. Pass out the paper. Keep a sheet for yourself.

Tell everyone to put two small tears in the paper, like this:

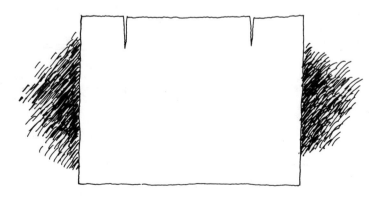

Or to save time you can make the tears before the show.

Announce that everyone is to hold the paper by the corners. Then, keeping their hands in place, they are to tear the paper into three pieces.

"You can't do it," you can say.

And you will be right. No matter how hard they try the paper will only tear in one place.

"Here's how it's done," you should announce. "Watch the great magician at work."

Clamp down on the middle section with your teeth. Then tear straight down. You'll end up with three pieces, one in each hand and one in your mouth.

Amazing!

Take a bow. Tell the audience you hope they've liked the show.

Enjoy the applause. You've earned it. Then, like a good magician, quickly disappear from the stage.

Chapter 9

◆

A Monster Feast

All the Creepy Creatures clapped. Henry had been right. He had put on a great magic show.

"You'll be seeing me again soon!" he said, saluting. "Seeing me on the cover of the *Creepy Creature Club Secrets of Scary Fun* book!"

"Don't count on it," said Rosa. "You didn't tell the readers how to do the floating-finger trick."

Henry snorted. "Now you're being impossible," he said. "Can't a magician have some secrets?"

"Maybe some," said Rosa. "But the floating finger is your best trick. We need to share it with the readers of this book."

"Sometimes sharing can be hard," said

Henry. "Even for someone like me, the world's greatest sharer."

"So are you going to tell us how to do the floating-finger trick?" asked Rosa.

"Let me think about it," said Henry.

"Fair enough," said Rosa. "In the meantime I'd like to share some of my scary recipes."

"Scary recipes?" said Melvin. He scratched his head. "What are those?"

"These," said Rosa. "I thought them all up myself."

Rosa's Creepy Creature Café

After a hard day's work monsters and monster lovers can build up a horrible hunger. When stomachs start growling—or worse yet, when the wolfman starts growling—better whip up a monster feast.

Almost any time is right for a Creepy Creature banquet. Halloween, of course, is best. But other times are good too. How about some Friday the thirteenth? Or what about a special birthday party for Count Dracula? Since no one knows on what day he was born, pick any date you want. Whatever the occasion, make it a special meal.

Decorate the dining room with your favorite monster mobiles and posters. Put down black crepe paper as your tablecloth. Do you have a plastic skull or pumpkin left over from Halloween? Put it in the middle of the table. In the zombie's favorite spot, the dead center.

Plan your menu carefully.

First make a list of the things you and your friends like to eat. Then think up horrible, creepy names for those tasty morsels. For instance, do you like hot dogs? If so, put them on your menu. But call them Roasted Giant's Fingers on a Bun.

Get an adult to help you prepare the meal. Never use the stove or an oven or other appliances without an adult present.

Pass out the menus before the meal is served. One look at the menu and maybe the guests will pass out too. Just be sure to wake them up before the meal comes.

They'll like what you have to serve, no matter what it is called.

Here are three menus from recent Creepy Creature monster feasts. Maybe they will give you some ideas for the best worst meal you and your friends have ever had.

The Creepy Creature Café

"Are You Brave Enough to Try Our Food?"

Today's Specials

Roasted Giant's Fingers on a Bun
(hot dogs)
Diced Fried Worms (french fries)
Blood Sauce (catsup)
Dracula Juice (tomato juice)
Eye Scream (vanilla ice cream topped
with cherries or grapes)

Doctor Frankenstein's Fine Foods

"A Meal You'll Always Remember—No Matter How Hard You Try to Forget It"

Bat Wings (chicken wings)
(Serve on a plate decorated with paper bats)

Shrunken, Fried UFOs (potato chips)

Vampire Soup (tomato soup)

Dried Spiders à la Mode (ice cream topped with raisins)

Count Dracula's Country Cooking

"Where the Food Isn't the Only Thing That Gets Bitten"

Snakes 'n' Cheese (macaroni and cheese)
Yummy Yuck (mashed potatoes with green food coloring)
Creamed Lizard Soup (split-pea soup)
The Blob (mixed lime and cherry gelatin dessert)

For an extra touch have your waiters dressed as monsters. After the meal, help clean up. Don't leave others with a monstrous mess.

As the French monsters say, bon appétit!

Chapter 10

◆

The Floating Finger, A Final Secret

When Rosa was finished, Henry stepped to the center of the room.

"Okay. I've made up my mind," he said. "I'll tell the floating-finger trick."

"Great. I'm glad you're going to share," said Rosa.

"Does this mean I'll be on the cover?" asked Henry.

"Maybe," said Rosa. "Maybe not. Remember, what's important is the sharing." Rosa narrowed her eyes. "I hope you're not doing this just to be famous."

"Of course not," said Henry. He shook his head and laughed. "Rosa, you are so right. Fame isn't what's important. Sharing is."

Everyone laughed. Everyone but Henry. "Hey, I'm serious," he said.

Everyone laughed again. And this time Henry did too.

"All right," he said. "Maybe I do want to be on the cover. And this is what's going to put me there. My fabulous floating-finger trick!"

Henry's Greatest Secret

Here's my all-time favorite trick. It's called the floating finger. Everything you need to make this trick work is close at hand. Very close. In fact, the only things you need are your two index fingers.

Do you want to see a finger float before your eyes?

You do? Then here is all you have to do:

Line up your index fingers horizontally a few inches in front of your eyes. Don't let them touch. Keep them about one-half inch apart.

Now focus your eyes just beyond the fingers.

Yuck! Do you see it? There, right between your two fingers. It's a short, fat,
floating finger. Don't look directly at it or it
will disappear. As long as you focus your
eyes beyond the fingers the ghostly finger
will remain.

Being scared is fun, as long as it is all in
fun. So what better way to end this book
than with a few of my favorite Creepy Creature riddles and jokes:

What insects are attracted to dead
flowers?
Zom-bees.

85

Monster #1: Why are you writing with that carrot?

Monster #2: Oh, no! I must have eaten my pencil.

Cannibal #1: Why were you fired from your job?

Cannibal #2: They caught me buttering up the boss.

Dr. Frankenstein: Can I take your pulse?

Patient: What's wrong? Haven't you got one of your own?

Papa Monster: How were the questions on the test?

Monster Son: They were easy.

Papa Monster: Then how come you got so many wrong?

Monster Son: The questions were easy. It was the answers that were hard.

That's it," said Henry, tipping his hat. "That's everything I know."

"You did a great job," said Rosa. "Really."

"Then that means I'll be on the cover?"

"We'll see," said Rosa.

"See when?" asked Henry.

"When the book comes out," said Rosa. "That's when you'll know."

Check out the cover. Did Henry get his wish?